MW01658031

Roller Coaster Ride

Story by Chris Bell
Illustrations by Julia Crouth

Rosie looked up at the roller coaster.
She held her ticket tightly
in her hand.

"Isn't this exciting?" yelled her dad.
He had to yell
over all the other noise
in the fun park.

Rosie nodded,
but inside, she felt scared.
She jumped when she heard
some children screaming
with excitement.

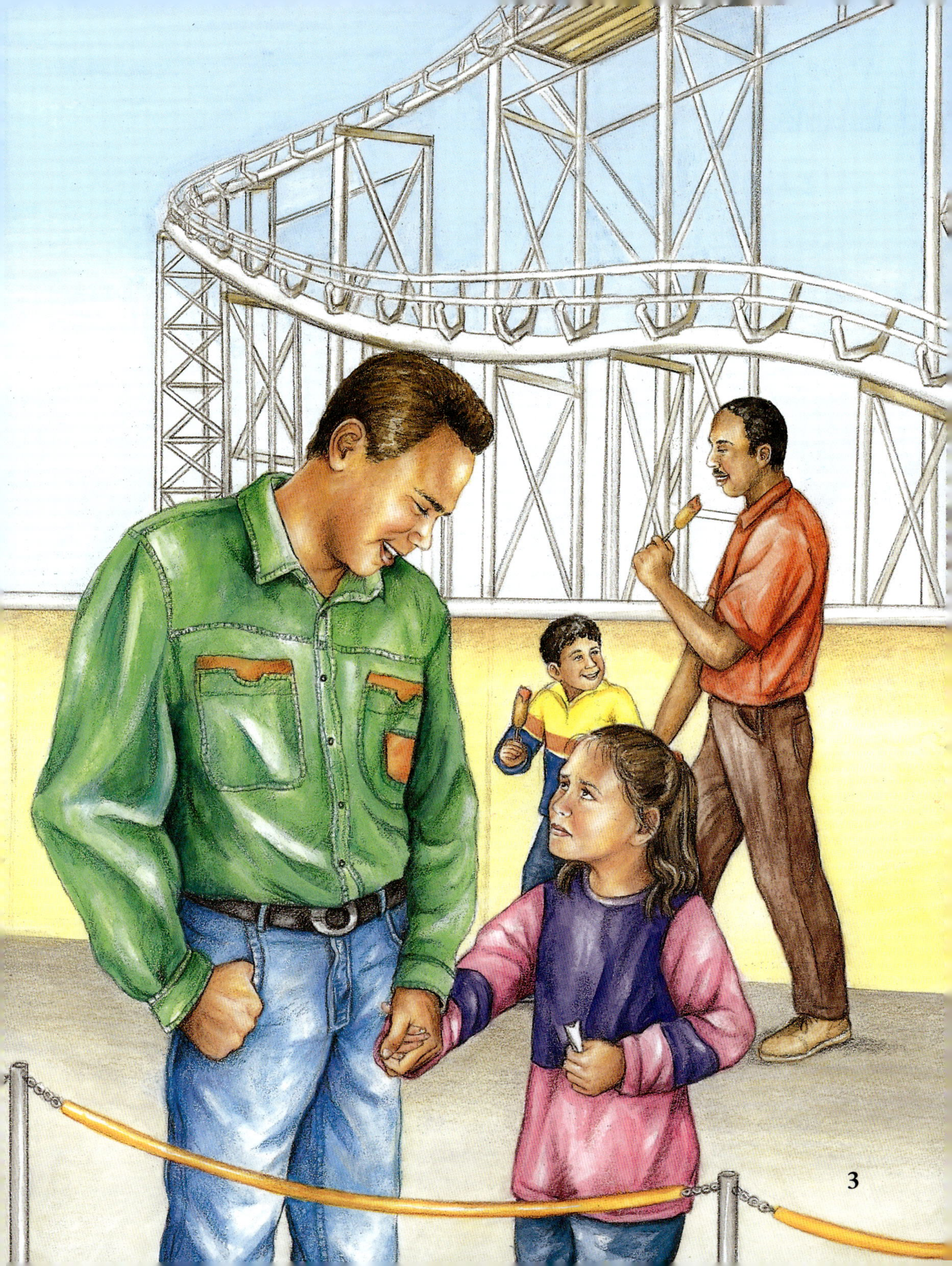

Another set of cars
flew down the track.
Rosie had never been on anything
that went as fast as this roller coaster.

"Do I still want a ride?"
she asked herself.
"What if I fall off?"

The noise grew louder and louder.
She could smell popcorn and hot dogs.

"What if I feel sick?"
she whispered to herself.

The next set of cars
came to a stop,
and the people climbed off.
Everyone in the line moved up.
Rosie and Dad would be next.

Rosie tugged at Dad's sleeve.
He bent down and she whispered,
"It's very high, isn't it?"

Dad laughed and nodded.
"We'll be able to see all the park from up there," he said.
"It will be just like flying."

Rosie didn't want to fly.
She didn't feel very well.

Then Dad said,
"Come on. It's our turn.
Here's our car."

Rosie tried to tell Dad
that she had changed her mind.

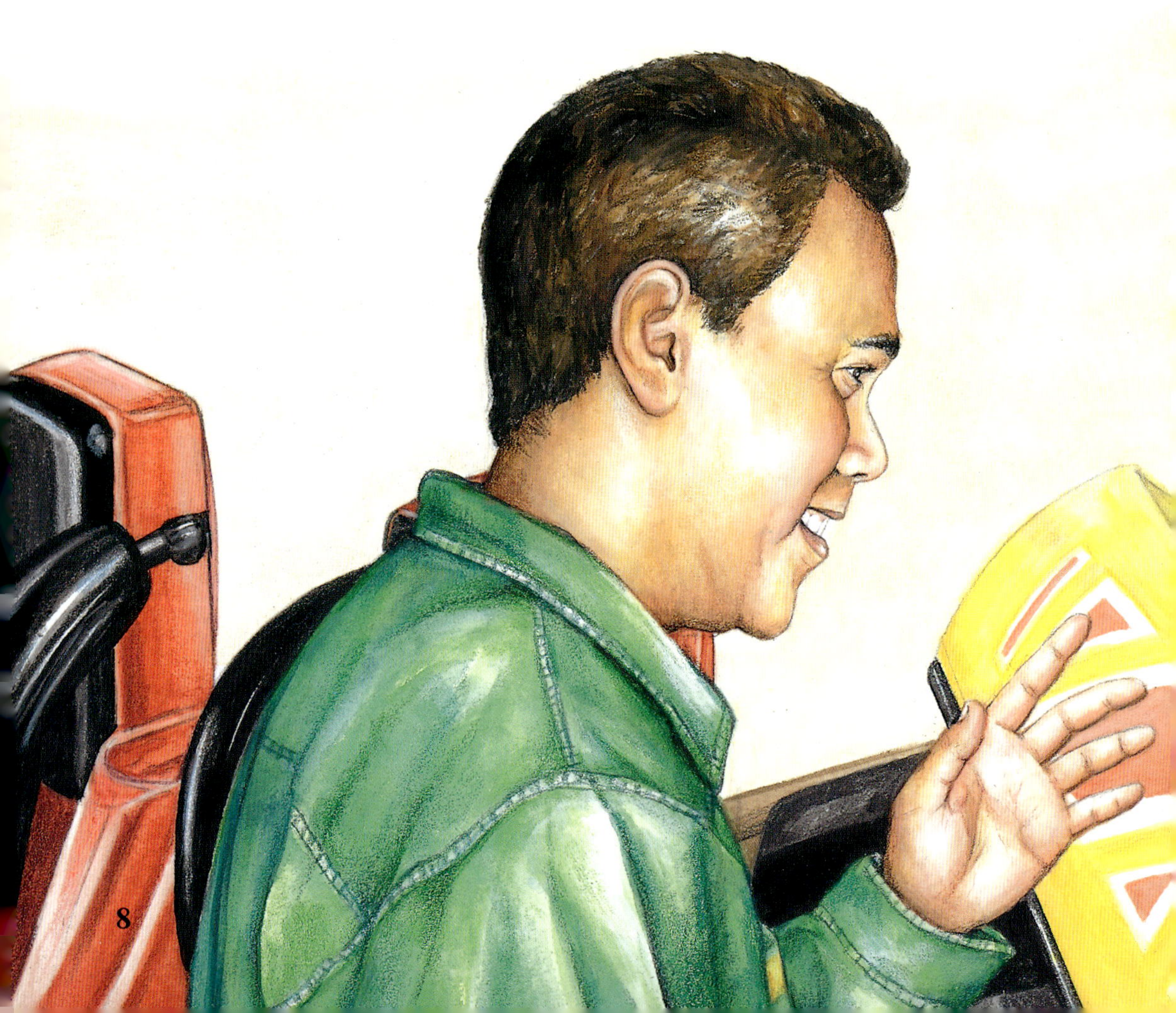

She opened her mouth
but no words came out.
Her legs were shaking
as she climbed into the car.

The car moved off slowly.

It's going to be all right,
thought Rosie.
I don't mind this sort of ride.
But then she looked at the tracks
ahead of her.
They seemed to go right up to the sky.

The car climbed higher
and higher.
When it reached the top,
Rosie looked down.
She could see bright colors
far below her.
Everything on the ground
looked small... very small!

The car was hardly moving.
Then it crept over the top of the hill.
Rosie looked down.
She gripped the safety bar
and closed her eyes.

The car flew down the tracks.
She felt the wind
rush through her hair.
Her stomach turned over
and she screamed.

But Dad was screaming
even louder!

When the car began to climb
the next hill, Rosie opened her eyes.
She didn't feel scared anymore.

"Isn't this exciting?"
she yelled to Dad.
But Dad didn't open his eyes.
He was terrified.

Rosie didn't notice.
She was having too much fun.
Every time the car
flew down another hill,
Rosie screamed with laughter.
She kept her eyes open
and felt the wind push her face
into funny shapes.

In no time at all, the ride was over
and the car came to a stop.

Rosie jumped out,
but Dad needed some help.
His eyes were still shut
and he looked sick.
He shook his head and said,
"Never again!"

Rosie grabbed his hand.
"Can we go on another ride,
please Dad?" she asked.
"And this time I want to go
on that one over there!"